(interceptpublishers@gmail.com)

ISBN: 978-1-9160441-2-8 (Paperback)
ISBN: 978-1-9160441-5-9 (eBook)

Typesetting and design by Pageset Ltd, High Wycombe, Buckinghamshire.
Printed and bound by Biddles Books Ltd, King's Lynn, Norfolk.

To the Red Cross nurse who became
my devoted wife for 49 years

Ernie

Edwardian Village Tales

As told by
'Ernie' Russell

illustrated by Janet Watson
edited by Andrew Russell

"We are all storytellers. We live in a network of stories.
There isn't a stronger connection between people than storytelling."

Jimmy Neil Smith, President, International Storytelling Centre

CONTENTS

STORYTELLERS

Oral storytelling is part of our civilisation. There have been many oral storytellers throughout history, often having a unique and intimate connection with their audiences. Some of the stories first told in Ancient Greece as early as the 6th Century BC, are still well known today, such as Aesop's fables, including, "The Boy Who Cried Wolf" and "The Tortoise and the Hare." His stories were not collected and written down for over 3 centuries after his death.

Some storytellers earned their living, travelling from town to town. Over time, the best storytellers have created new stories, using the same characters. Some storytellers added a new twist to an old story to keep things interesting, but the characters' personalities largely remained the same. The characters had to remain the same. In fact, nothing else would have been acceptable, because the people who heard the stories believed they were true!

'Ernie' was a storyteller in this tradition.

Ernest William Russell, born 22nd January 1893, Seisdon, Staffordshire

THIS STORYTELLER

In his later life 'Ernie' Russell wrote about his life in great detail, some 120,000 words, which are being published separately (see inside back page for details).

Born in 1893, he grew up in rural Staffordshire (Pattingham, Seisdon and Trysull). The family emigrated to Canada, but he came back to fight in The Great War. He then married the nurse who tended his wounds. He also wrote in great detail about his career as the land agent for Bedfordshire County Council, including his role in World War 2.

The storyteller in this book makes no claims to literary importance and, in fact, some of these stories have never been written down until now. In the best oral storytelling tradition, some may have been handed down from generations past. It is most likely that some of the tales recorded in this publication are not based on fact, or were 'borrowed' from other storytellers. Many others actually happened to the storyteller, or have a unique feel to them which suggests they probably occurred. Of course, over the years there will have been added elements of theatrics, improvisation and embellishment.

Are these tales entertaining, educational, for cultural preservation, or even instilling moral values in those who have heard them over the past 100 plus years? 'Ernie' will let you make up your own mind. They can certainly be seen as an insight into his life, the family and life in parts of some small villages in rural Staffordshire well over 100 years ago.

THE ILLUSTRATOR

If you had asked the ten-year-old Janet what she wanted to do when she grew up,

“Be an artist” was the answer.

However, over the next few years this changed into studying for a degree in art history, followed by a museum studies diploma.

It led me to work in museums in Glasgow, Lancaster and Inverness, where I have now lived for over 25 years. Throughout this time, I have enjoyed drawing and painting in watercolours, with a particular interest in botanical art, as my love of gardening developed.

On being asked to undertake the illustrations for this book my first thoughts were about the distance between the Scottish Highlands and rural south Staffordshire and then the challenge of drawing people and animals – very different from plants!

The first step was to get a sense of place and period. For this the internet proved an invaluable resource once I got over my technical phobias. Research was great fun and included such obscure byways as whether hand pumps for beer were used in those times.

The stories handed down in the Russell family are charming and illustrate a bygone age. I hope the drawings have captured some of the humour and character of a certain time and place – and achieved that ten-year old’s ambition.

Janet Watson

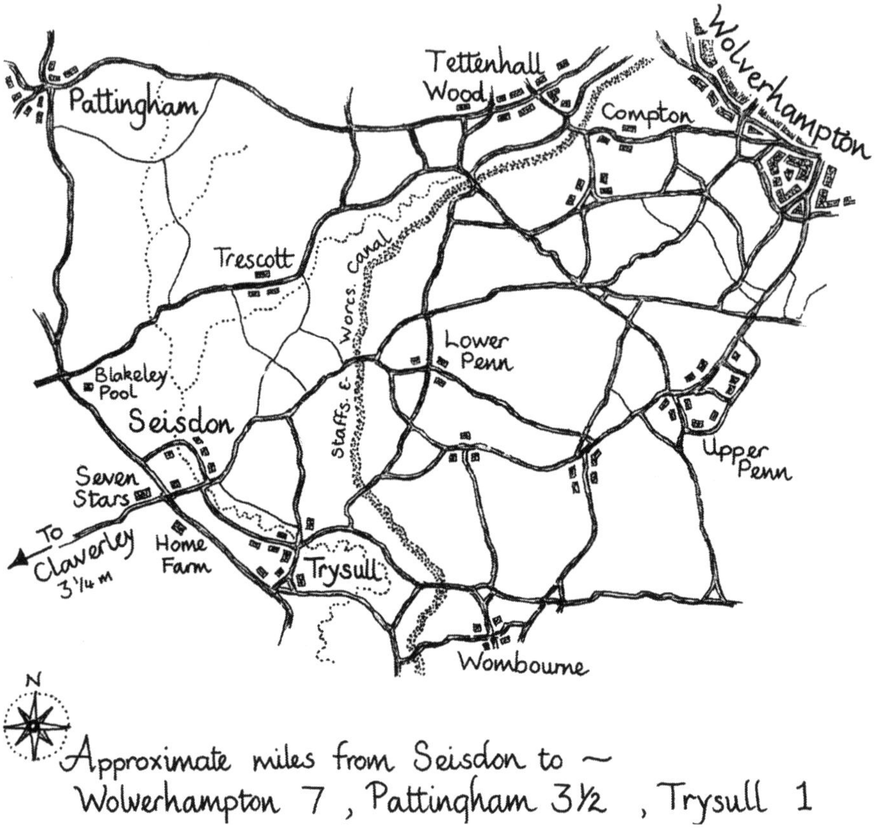

Map drawn by book illustrator Janet Watson

THE SETTING FOR THESE 'TALES'

The setting for these illustrated tales is rural Staffordshire, UK, close to Wolverhampton, but it might be unwise to think they could only have happened in this part of the world.

This map of the area is based on various historical sources and shows the small geographic area that Ernie Russell was raised in, the pony and trap tracks (there were few roads in those Edwardian times) ...... and most importantly for many of the characters mentioned in this book, the location of their local meeting place, the Seven Stars public house!

Seven Stars Public House, Seisdon

1. INTRODUCTION

My Grandfather, William Russell, (known throughout the family and generally as Grandfather Russell) was already quite an old man during the dying years of the 19th century.

He was evidently a likeable, old rogue, who liked a drop or two to drink occasionally (more about that later), but also had a lifetime of scurrilous stories about many of the inhabitants of Seisdon (our village) and the surrounding farmlands of the English West Midlands.

Although Grandfather Russell was born and bred in foreign parts (in the next village of Pattingham, a good three miles away to the north), he was a popular member of the Seven Star's coterie in Seisdon.

He and his wife ('Granny' to all the family) had moved to Seisdon from Pattingham a few years previously after closing down his cobbler's shop when his son (my father) offered him the tenancy of Blakeley Pool farm, a smallholding, which lay between the two villages.

One of Grandfather Russell's favourite stories, which he told regularly in the public bar of the Seven Stars (the one and only public house in Seisdon), concerned a well-to-do, local, farming family, although one always had to take his stories with a large pinch of salt. It went something like this:

2. A FAMILY STORY

A very well thought of gentleman and his wife, who lived in one of the larger houses in the village, were blessed with a very promising son. In due course, the son grew to manhood.

One day he came to his father and said,

"Dad, Isobel White and I have become very good friends and we are so attached to each other that we would like to get married."

The father looked sadly at his son and said,

"My boy, I am so sorry to hear this, because you can't marry Isobel White – you see, she is really your sister."

The young man was shocked and disappointed but gradually forgot about Isobel.

About a year later, he went to his father again and said

"Dad, Daphne Brown and I have become very much attached to each other and would like to get married."

The father looked at him and said,

"Oh dear! Oh dear! I am very sorry about this. I am afraid you will not be able to marry Daphne either; you see, she is also your sister."

The son was naturally very upset indeed about this, so much so that he decided he must tell his mother. Thus, he went to his mother and told her how he had become very attached to these two girls, but whom he could not marry because they were really his sisters. His mother put her arms around him and said,

"My boy, you need not worry yourself about this. You see, he is not really your father!"

All Saints' Church, Trysull, Staffordshire

3. OUR VILLAGE

Our village in those days consisted of two small groups of houses, each clustered around an intersection of country lanes and separated from each other by a long, fairly straight, main street.

This narrow road linked the two parts of the parish and led from the Seven Stars hostelry, the hub of village life on weekdays. The small, mediaeval parish church, its squat, brown, sandstone body with the low tower and tidy, well-filled churchyard, dominated the village in so many important ways.

The villagers were still, as for so many centuries beforehand, baptised, married and buried within its boundaries.

The Vicar, in charge of all these comings and goings, was a powerful figure in the village and lived in the Vicarage, an imposing, ivy- covered, dull-red-brick house, which stood in its own large garden, just across School Lane from the church.

School Lane led up to the newly constructed, red-brick school, with its own playground, which replaced a small outhouse attached to the schoolmaster's house, which had served for many years as a schoolroom.

Mr. Salmon, the Schoolmaster, ruled the village children with a kindly rod of iron. I was born in 1893 and attended school in the village. The next story is about this schoolmaster and my early school days.

Aa Bb
One good turn
deserves another
45
×9
58
×6
237
+185

4. THE SCHOOLMASTER

One lovely, crisp, autumn morning, I was walking along the country lanes to school with some friends, the sons of workers on my father's farm. To make the long journey more interesting and to put off any thoughts of the day's labours to come, we played football on the way using a small india- rubber ball, pretending that we were playing for our local team, Wolverhampton Wanderers. Sometimes we played in the direction of school, but equally often in the opposite direction.

Suddenly, someone shouted that we were going to be very late for school. We all knew that this would mean serious trouble from Mr Salmon, when we arrived.

I don't know whose brilliant idea it was, but we decided to pack the inside of the shoulders of our jackets with handfuls of grass plucked from the roadside banks. We thought that this padding would protect us to some extent, when the Schoolmaster used his cane across our shoulders, as we fully expected him to do. We duly arrived at the school in a hot, flustered condition and very late indeed.

As soon as we entered the schoolroom, we were lined up, without a word, to receive our well-deserved punishment. This, we thought, is where our padded shoulder pieces would come in useful.

However, we were astonished when Mr Salmon told us to hold out our hands, and each of us received a good lashing on our hands. With a twinkle in his eyes, the Schoolmaster then ordered us to go outside and empty the grass from our jackets before settling down to the morning's lessons.

"Our village" – looking towards All Saints' Church, Trysull, Staffordshire

5. SOME VILLAGE PEOPLE

As will be described in the next chapter, the villagers were strongly class conscious and it was realised that everyone was born to a certain station in life.

The villagers were allocated to a particular class at birth; their future place in society having already been determined by their breeding (i.e. inherited family wealth and importance in society) and financial status of the parents and other relatives. There were three members of the gentry (i.e. not quite members of the aristocracy) in our village at the end of the nineteenth century.

The most important of the three was the village squire, Mr George Aston-Pudsey, who lived in the large, imposing, stone-built Hall, which stood at the end of a long drive through parkland; there was a pillared, gated entrance to the drive in the village's main street.

The Squire's brother, Mr. William Aston, lived in a smaller, but nonetheless impressive residence, further along the same street. It was slightly nearer the Seven Stars public house, but further away from the church, as befitted his slightly lower rank in society. His house was built sturdily of dark-red brick, in the Georgian style. The extensive grounds were separated from the road (and from the prying eyes of the villagers) by a high brick wall, in which were set large double gates of patterned wrought iron.

Through the gate, one could see an area of well-tended lawns inside a circular driveway, which was flanked on one side by outbuildings comprising the coach house and stables.

6. THE ASTON FAMILY

Readers will doubtless be puzzled by the fact that two of the most respected members of the village community, Mr. George Aston-Pudsey and Mr. William Aston, had different family names, although they were brothers.

Such confusion is entirely understandable, but the reason for the different surnames is really very simple. You see, Mr George married a Miss Pudsey and, as a condition of the marriage, he had to take her name so that he became Mr. George Aston-Pudsey rather than plain Mr. George Aston. The reason for this, I believe, was to ensure that the bride's family name of Pudsey would be perpetuated even in the absence of male heirs. It seems that the Pudseys for several generations had shown a preponderance of daughters, but a distinct paucity of boys.

In due course Mr. George Aston-Pudsey and his wife produced their one and only offspring. As was to be expected, it was a girl.

I have been told that this daughter, Miss Lavinia Aston-Pudsey, eventually married a partner in a firm of solicitors with offices in a nearby small town, where a well-known firm of estate agents still flourishes under the name of Doolittle and Dalley.

This solicitor, I believe, a Mr. Nicholas Parkinson, had to change his name too, on marriage, becoming Mr. Nicholas Parkinson-Aston-Pudsey, which Granny said was quite a mouthful!

7. MR. WILLIAM BARTON

The third member of the village gentry was Mr. William Barton, who lived in a large, brick-built mansion, beyond the Seven Stars public house. This house was also Georgian and had behind it a large stabling block which housed several thoroughbred horses and kennels for his hounds.

Mr. Barton was a bon-viveur and a very active member of the local Hunt. Mr. Barton often used to tell the following story about one of his forefathers who lived in the village many years ago.

This Mr. Barton of a bygone age used to enjoy visits from one or other of his farm tenants, particularly during the long, winter evenings. They did themselves very well indeed on such occasions and the beer and wine flowed freely. After one such convivial evening with a farmer called Brown, the latter set off from Mr. Barton's house in the early hours of the morning, and made his way slowly and unsteadily homewards by the light of his lantern.

Early next morning, Mr. Brown was very surprised when his housekeeper woke him, as it was far too early after such a long and tiring evening.

She handed him a note from Mr. Barton, his host of the previous evening.

The note read as follows,

"Dear Brown, I very much enjoyed your visit yesterday evening. My man, who has delivered this note to you, is returning your lantern, with my thanks. Will you please send back with him my parrot and cage, which evidently guided you home safely this morning."

8. THE REST OF THE VILLAGERS

The rest of the village consisted of houses and cottages of various sizes. The 'gentlemen' (i e. those few fortunate enough to have an independent income) and the one or two professional people, for example the local doctor and horse doctor (later to become known as veterinarians), lived in modest, but well-kept, houses, each set in its own plot of land.

Most of the other villagers, including the artisans and some of the farm workers, lived in rows of cottages, some of them thatched, scattered throughout the village.

On the outskirts of Seisdon were several farms, the tenants of which rented their farm holdings from wealthy landowners. My father and Grandfather Russell were two of these tenant farmers, the former of the large, mainly arable farm, Home Farm and the latter eking out a living (mostly with Granny's help) from the much smaller Blakeley Pool farm.

Grandfather Russell had never really cared much for hard physical work and, as he grew older, his smallholding became ever more neglected. Fortunately, Granny kept some poultry, and much of their income came from selling eggs at the local market in Wolverhampton.

Grandfather Russell took the eggs to market each Wednesday morning in the pony and trap; this was a job he never minded doing, because it gave him the opportunity of stopping at one or two pubs on the way back, away from Granny's watchful eyes.

My father told me the following tale about what happened to Grandfather Russell on his way back from market one summer evening.

9. TRAPPED

Grandfather Russell was well known to imbibe strong drink very freely indeed on occasions, particularly before returning home in his pony and trap from the local market town on market day.

One market day some of his friends from the Seven Stars decided to have a little bit of fun with him. They knew that their friend would visit one or two hostelries on the way home and that he would be so bemused by what he had been drinking, that he would go to sleep sitting on the seat of the trap and let his pony find the way home.

Well, on this occasion, the friends closed the gate leading to Blakeley Pool farm and waited nearby for Grandfather Russell to return.

Sure enough, along came the pony and trap with the driver fast asleep at the reins. When the pony stopped at the closed gate, the friends very quietly took the pony out of the shafts of the trap and led her through the gate.

After closing the gate again, they threaded the shafts of the trap between the bars of the gate, put the pony back in the shafts again and went home to bed.

When Grandfather Russell awoke in the early hours of the morning, he was mystified to find his pony on one side of the gate and the trap on the other.

Granny was not amused when he finally returned home!

Burdas Cottage, Clive Road, Pattingham, Staffordshire

10. THE VILLAGE HIERARCHY

Members of the village community before the turn of the century were, as I have mentioned before, ranked or graded in a very definite, usually unchanging order, according to their breeding, wealth or calling.

It was, for example, very noticeable that the three village members of the gentry, namely Messrs. George Aston-Pudsey, William Aston and William Barton, all of them gentlemen farmers and wealthy landowners, were considered to be a cut or two above all the others, even the Vicar.

Lower down the social scale, but not much (at least in their own estimation), came the Vicar and the professional people, such as the doctor, and those (such as Gentleman Perry) who had an independent income, so that they were not obliged to work for a living.

The next set consisted of the tenant farmers, including my father, and the Schoolmaster, the respected and well-liked Mr. John Salmon. This group was not rich, or of independent means, as were those in the higher echelons of society, but were hardworking and, in many ways, the backbone of the community.

Slightly lower down the social scale were such worthies as the landlord of the Seven Stars, the village policeman and the craftsmen, such as the cabinet (and coffin) maker, the shoemaker, and the farm foremen and managers.

11. THE LOWER ORDERS

The lowest stratum of all, apart from the itinerant, seasonal workers, who had not even one foot on the social ladder, were the employed persons: the farm workers, the carpenters, the draymen, the domestic servants and so on.

Everyone in the village knew their place in society in those days, but there was apparently little jealousy or bitterness against those placed in a higher stratum of society; rather there was a feeling of superiority (and responsibility) within all groups towards those less fortunate than themselves.

In particular, those who were lucky enough to inherit a high position in the village hierarchy generally also inherited a deep sense of duty towards their fellows, particularly those in other, lower strata. Was this such a bad system, my father asked me one day.

My father once told me the following story about Mr. William Aston and Mr. William Barton, which nicely illustrates the feelings of some villagers towards members of the landed gentry.

12. MEN OF SUBSTANCE

Although Mr. William Aston was the Squire's brother and was a prominent member of the village community, he lived frugally, always maintaining that he was quite a poor man. However, many of the villagers doubted this and generally regarded him as a man of considerable wealth.

Nearly everybody agreed that he was not as well off as Mr. William Barton, who lived lavishly and, what is more, employed a groom-gardener, kept three hunting horses and a small pack of hounds. He hunted three or four days each week during the season and organised large shooting parties, at which he provided hospitality on the grand scale.

Most villagers, with the notable exception of Granny, therefore regarded him as a very rich man, who would leave a fortune when he died.

When eventually the two men passed on in the early years of this century, however, most people got a surprise. Mr. William Aston left about £70,000 in his will, a very considerable sum in those days, and probably worth more than four times as much at today's values.

Mr. William Barton, on the other hand, who had always lived as if he had plenty of money, died almost penniless.

Granny, who didn't like either of them very much, was wiser and more astute than most. She had predicted this situation many years before, when she was heard to remark to Grandfather Russell, after she had had an altercation with Mr. Barton, that the latter would die in a ditch as a poor man. She had also said on several occasions that Mr. William Aston was a "bit of a skinflint" with all his money.

13. GRANNY AND MR. BARTON

Granny's dislike of Mr. Barton went back many years. Although he was a churchwarden and a pillar of village society, she thought he was 'stuck up' and never lost an opportunity to show him that she was at least as good as he was.

One warm summer's morning, just as Granny was pegging out the washing on the line, Mr. William Barton, whose large farm adjoined Grandfather Russell's much smaller Blakeley Pool farm, stopped his pony and trap just outside the yard fence of the small farmhouse.

He called across to Granny in a loud voice,

"Mrs Russell, I want you to keep your chickens out of my field of barley."

Granny, not to be outdone, retorted,

"Mr. Barton, I want you to keep your sheep out of my meadow."

Mr. Barton was nonplussed at being spoken to in this way and drove away without another word!

14. GENTLEMAN PERRY

The case of the two Mr. Perrys further illustrates the distinction that existed between the classes of society in our village. There were two Mr. Perrys in Seisdon, when I was a young boy at the turn of the century.

Although they lived almost directly opposite one another, on the main village street, they were not related and belonged to quite different strata of the village hierarchy.

One lived in a fairly large house and was comparatively well off, being of independent means; he was known universally as 'Gentleman Perry'.

The other Mr. Perry, who lived in a small house opposite his namesake, was a smallholder, keeping a few cows and growing a few vegetables for sale at Wolverhampton market. He was known as 'Walter Perry'.

It was very noticeable that the villagers always treated 'Gentleman Perry' with considerably more respect than Walter Perry.

This emphasises once again the importance that the villagers attached to the birthright and wealth of the other residents, even if they did have the same name.

1ST
PLUM
1ST
1ST

15. THE COLONEL

Colonel Nickerson-Smith (Indian Army, retired) considered himself almost at the top of the social hierarchy. Indeed, he was used to being in authority and was very comfortably off.

Although the villagers outwardly treated him with appropriate respect, they found him a bit overbearing and secretly their thoughts about him were anything but respectful. He was Chairman of the committee that organised the Village Show each summer.

He always chose himself to be Chief Judge at the annual flower, fruit and vegetable competition and to present the prizes afterwards. The villagers generally accepted this self-nomination with good grace, because he did not exhibit any produce himself and he was considered to be above bribery.

He also donated a generous sum to the expenses of the Show, and his cook provided most of the excellent food that was available to exhibitors and spectators alike in the tea tent.

The main drawback, as far as the villagers were concerned, was that the Colonel insisted on making a long speech, mainly about his military exploits in India, before presenting the prizes. The audience, which was much more interested in finding out who had won the various prizes, usually became rather restless at this point.

Although the Colonel always considered himself to be a shy and retiring man, Dick Gregory, the village wag, was convinced that he liked the sound of his own voice far too much. Gregory said to a pal in the Seven Stars one day,

"The Colonel reminds me of Mr. Aston's prize ram – never happier than when he's on his hind legs."

16. THE PARISH OVERSEERS

The social standing of individual members varied greatly even within the same stratum of society. In other words, there was a definite pecking order between individuals in the various groups, whether gentry, gentlemen, professional people, tenant farmers, artisans, farmworkers or domestic servants.

The status of my father in the group of Seisdon's small farmers must have been fairly high, because he was appointed one of the Parish Overseers, a very prestigious position in the village community. The Clerk of the Overseers was the Schoolmaster, Mr. John Salmon.

My father explained to me that the main duty of the Overseers was to see that the local rating system, whereby money was raised locally through a kind of land tax, was carried out fairly and efficiently. They did not set the level of these taxes, but had to ensure that the dues were collected on time.

This latter duty perhaps explained why so many people appeared to be out when my father called!

St Chad's Church, Pattingham, Staffordshire

17. THE PARISH CHURCH AND VICARAGE

The village social hierarchy even extended into the activities of the parish church, which occupied such an important geographical and spiritual position in Seisdon. At the top of the parish church hierarchy was undoubtedly the vicar, or parson, who was nearly always a university man.

He was always highly regarded by the villagers, partly because he was a holy man (but not necessarily without his little weaknesses) and partly because of his academic training, deep knowledge and wisdom. Such was their esteem that the vicar of the day ranked equally, or almost so, with the landed gentry of the community.

The duties of a country parson were generally not onerous in those days and there was plenty of time for contemplation and the enjoyment of the good things of life. The vicars of Seisdon parish were, therefore, usually content with their lot and, accordingly, lived to a ripe old age. Because changes in the incumbents were few and far between, it was not unusual for the same vicar to baptise, confirm, marry and bury the same individuals. It was traditional in our village for the two churchwardens to be drawn from the small group of wealthy gentleman farmers. When I was a small boy, Mr. William Aston and Mr. William Barton occupied these vital offices.

The reserved pews for the churchwardens and their families served almost as a badge of rank among the parishioners lower down the scale. Without pews specially reserved for them were the three or four sidesmen, of which my father was one.

I believe that my grandmother belonged to the Flower Arrangers Circle, but no women were ever allowed to become churchwardens or sidesmen in those days – such a thing was quite unthinkable.

The sidesmen were invariably chosen from the professional men or the more senior members of the tenant farmer group. Mr. John Salmon, the schoolmaster, was both organist and choirmaster. As I was in the church choir from the age of seven years, I was not only under Mr. Salmon's benevolent but watchful eye on schooldays, but also on Sundays and at choir practice.

I gleaned many stories from my father and from Grandfather Russell about the incumbents of Seisdon and neighbouring parishes. Grandfather Russell, unlike his only son, was not a regular churchgoer and greatly enjoyed poking fun at the clergy. He always said that he was relying on his more sanctimonious relatives to put in a good word for him at the Gates of Heaven.

Here follows a few of their favourite tales concerning the clergy.

18. THE VICARAGE GARDEN

The local parson was sitting in his study one morning, preparing his sermon for next Sunday, when he heard a lot of noise coming from the vicarage garden. He went to the window to see what was going on.

His gardener was scaring some pigeons away from the vegetables. He was shouting loudly at the birds,

"Shoooo.... Shoooo.... Bugger off!"

The parson was a bit disturbed by the use of such bad language in his garden and decided that he should go out and have a word with the gardener.

He opened the garden door and approached the gardener.

"John," he said, "There's no need to swear at the birds like that. Just say ....

Shoooo.... Shoooo... and they will bugger off."

19. GOOD EVENING, VICAR

Grandfather Russell used to tell about a bachelor vicar of a neighbouring parish, who liked sometimes to invite some of his friends to the vicarage for a convivial evening. On such occasions, he and his guests would first eat a good dinner and then enjoy a few glasses of wine together, while swapping experiences and stories.

The parson's housekeeper, an angular and stern spinster, prepared the meal and left it heating on the hob, before departing for the night to her lonely and comfortless cottage in the village. She strongly disapproved of her employer's weakness for wine and did all she could to keep him from having too much to drink.

One evening, the vicar invited one of his churchwardens to dinner. The housekeeper, in an attempt to prevent the evening from becoming too convivial, hid all the cups, tumblers and wineglasses before she left after preparing the dinner.

After they had eaten an excellent meal, the parson fetched out a bottle of wine from the sideboard, but could find nothing from which to drink it. He did not want to ask his esteemed guest to drink from the bottle, so he apologised for not being able to offer him any wine.

"Never mind, Vicar," said the churchwarden,

"We don't need wineglasses. I can see some eggshells in the fireplace. Let us use those instead."

When the housekeeper returned the next morning, she was very puzzled to find two large pieces of eggshell and an empty wine bottle on the dining table!

20. GOOD MORNING, VICAR

The same parson quite often liked to visit some of his farmer friends in his parish in the evenings.

On such occasions he would stay with them quite a while and there is no doubt that more than a little imbibing of intoxicants took place.

After one evening visit of this kind, the vicar was returning to his vicarage in the early hours, following a very convivial evening indeed. Dawn was breaking over the rolling farmland to the east when he met one of the local farmworkers in the lane.

He thought that this man needed some appropriate moral guidance.

"You know, Sam," said the vicar, "you really shouldn't be out at this time of night."

Sam looked rather surprised. What the parson did not realise was that this farmworker was actually on his way to give his team of horses their early morning feed!

21. "GOOD FRIENDS IS BEST APART"

Dick Gregory had a brother Jim, who was also a bit of a character. One day, when Jim was doing a bit of odd-jobbing for Grandfather on his farm, he explained to me that there had been some difficulties within the Gregory family – in fact it seemed to me that there had been a good old family row, no doubt involving fisticuffs.

I don't know what it was all about, but both Dick and Jim displayed what looked remarkably like bruises on their faces for some time afterwards.

"You know," remarked Jim Gregory philosophically,

"Good friends and relatives is best apart."

22. OUR FAMILY

My father, who rented Home Farm, Seisdon, from the squire, Mr. George Aston-Pudsey, was a pillar of village society, a staunchly religious man and a stern parent.

He was not nearly as easy-going as his father, Grandfather Russell, although he, too, took a drink or two occasionally, particularly at haymaking and harvest-time, when he was helping his men in the fields, as for example, in the following story.

23. THE HAYMAKERS

When I was a boy, just before the turn of the century, it was the custom in our village for the farm workers to drink plenty of beer in the field at haymaking time. The beer quenched their thirst and helped to relieve their aching muscles.

One day, my mother suggested that I should go and watch father and one of his men, Watkins, making hay in a distant field. I trotted happily along the rutted farm track in the warm sunshine.

I have been told that when he saw me approaching, father turned to Watkins and said,

"Here comes my boy. I hope that he is not bringing bad news of some kind."

Watkins looked up from raking the hay and, shading his eyes, replied,

"Looks like there's two of them."

My father looked again, also shading his eyes,

"So there are, I wonder who the other boy is?"

Obviously, father and Watkins had been indulging themselves with refreshing beer to such an extent that they were seeing double!

24. BROTHERLY LOVE

On another occasion, my younger brother, Charlie, lost his sandwiches on the way to our school and, as a result, had nothing to eat until he got home at teatime.

I had my sandwiches to eat, so I was all right. Later that evening, I was accompanying father in his horse and trap to visit a farmer friend in the next parish.

For something to say, I told my father that Charlie had lost his sandwiches on his way to school.

My father said,

"Oh, I am sorry to hear that, but I am sure that you shared your sandwiches with him."

I replied,

"Oh, no, father, they were my sandwiches and I thought that I had better eat them."

Without a word, father stopped the trap, caught hold of me and I was pushed out on to the road.

During my long walk home in the gathering dusk, I had plenty of time to reflect on my selfishness and on father's ability to mete out rough justice.

25. STOLEN APPLES ARE SWEET

On yet another occasion, I was playing soccer with some of my friends from the village school, when we thought it would be a good thing to raid Mr. Aston-Pudsey's apple orchard, which adjoined the Hall.

We went up a quiet cart track, which ran alongside the high brick wall fronting the orchard, and climbed over. We ran over to the trees with the rosiest apples and started throwing sticks up at the branches to dislodge the fruit, collecting the fallen apples in our school caps.

We had been enjoying ourselves like this for several minutes, but then realised that we were being observed. Standing a little way off was Mr. George Aston-Pudsey himself, looking intently at what we boys were doing. He said nothing, with all of us rushing for the wall, over which we disappeared like greased lightning.

Mr. Aston-Pudsey was not only the Squire, he was also the landlord of Home Farm, and, accordingly, my father was his tenant. I was, therefore, expecting trouble.

Nothing was said to me about this episode for a couple of days. I was even beginning to think that the Squire had not recognised me. I was not to be so lucky, because, one afternoon soon after, father called me into the house from the garden, where I was playing, and gave me a sound thrashing.

I have to say that I could not look an apple in the face for a long time, but, on reflection, I realised from that time on that crime really does not pay.

26. SACKCLOTH AND ASHES

I have already mentioned Grandfather Russell several times. He was full of amusing stories about other folks, but he was himself the subject of numerous tales.

My Uncle Harry (Chesterfield) used to say that Grandfather Russell was generally quite abstemious, although, it had to be admitted, he occasionally had a little too much to drink.

Even when he was over 80 years old, for example, he would go for quite a while, even two or three weeks at a time without intoxicants.

Suddenly, and for no apparent reason, for a few days he would take to whisky – or something else, if his favourite drink was not available.

During these bouts he would be even more cheery and talkative than usual, although Granny tried to keep him in the house as much as possible.

After such lapses, he was so regretful that, as Uncle Harry put it, he would put on sackcloth and ashes

...... until the next time.

27. GRANDFATHER

Grandfather Russell was nearly 80 years old when he occasionally stayed at Home Farm for a few days, mainly to give Granny a rest and to allow her to do some spring-cleaning.

On one of these visits, he decided to walk across the fields to the village just before noon. While he was there, he naturally visited the Seven Stars public house to see some of his cronies and to have a few drinks.

It was such a lovely afternoon, when he emerged from the hostelry, that he decided to take a roundabout route back to Home Farm.

On the way, he felt so drowsy and at peace with the world, possibly because of what he had had to drink, that he entered a gateway at the side of the lane and lay down in the warm sunshine. He fell fast asleep, with a very happy expression on his face.

The folk back at the farm became worried when Grandfather Russell did not return for his mid-day meal; even more so when closing time at the Seven Stars had passed. The whole family was turned out to look for him, but it was more than two hours later that my father found him sleeping peacefully behind the hedge, a happy smile still playing on his face.

We didn't have the heart to tell Granny about this escapade.

28. A PRESENT FOR GRANDAD

During the First World War Grandfather Russell, who at that time was getting on for 80 years of age, lived with Granny in a cottage on the edge of the village.

As the rest of the family had left Seisdon to farm in Canada, I spent one of my leaves from the WW1 trenches in France in this tiny cottage. There was only one bedroom and I had to share a large feather bed with Grandfather Russell. Granny was relegated to a small camp bed in the corner of the same room. I had with me a bottle of whisky as a present and this was promptly hidden from view by the old man.

During the first night at the cottage, Grandfather Russell, moving about on his side of the bed, wakened me. This was followed by a gurgling sound as the old man swallowed some of the whisky.

I said,

"What are you doing, Granddad?"

He replied in a low, hoarse voice,

"Hold your hush."

This was a term he used when he didn't want Granny to know what he was up to.

He gurgled some more, turned over and went to sleep.

Granny, in her own little bed, didn't hear any of this or, if she did, she never let on that she had.

29. READY-MONEY TOM

One of Grandfather Russell's brothers was known in the district as 'Ready-Money Tom' (Thomas).

He was a hay and straw dealer, visiting farms in his pony and trap to buy hay and straw for selling to other farmers, who lacked sufficient fodder and bedding for their own livestock.

He always carried around with him a bag of gold sovereigns, attached to his belt; this bag used to jingle a bit as he walked.

This reminded his clients that he carried cash on his person and that he was always prepared to pay cash on the nail for any deal that was agreed.

This always worked to his advantage and enabled him to strike the best bargain, because the astute farmers always reckoned that 'a bird in hand is worth two in the bush'.

Ready-Money Tom was thus able to buy his hay and straw cheaply, but, it was said, he always charged a lot for it when it was sold.

SIX
PENCE
1907

30. COUSIN JOHN

'Ready-Money Tom' had two sons, both farmers, who lived a few miles away from our village. One of these sons was called Jesse, who farmed in the next parish, kept a large flock of sheep and was fairly prosperous. His wife and he had no children and Jesse was generally considered to be extremely careful with his money, as indeed was his father Tom.

Granny said that Jesse was a miser.

His brother, John, was quite different, a happy man with little money but with a doting wife and a happy swarm of children.

One market day, when I must have been about fourteen years old, I was at Wolverhampton market with my father, when we met Jesse Russell. We all shook hands and exchanged the usual pleasantries and this was followed by a discussion of the depressed state of the market prices.

As my cousin turned to go, I was delighted when he stopped, put his hand in his pocket and drew out a silver sixpence.

I was handed the coin with the admonishment,

"Don't spend it all at once," as he waved and strode away down the narrow street. As soon as Cousin Jesse was out of earshot my father said to me,

"Look after that carefully, Ernie, and get it framed. I have never known him to give money away before."

31. GRANNY AND READY-MONEY TOM

I have already mentioned Granny Russell's outspoken ways. She never minced her words, particularly with relatives.

One day her brother-in-law, Thomas Russell (known locally as 'Ready-Money Tom'), expressed interest in buying Grandfather Russell's paddock, which was just across the road from their cottage.

Granny was well aware of Thomas's reputation for buying cheaply and selling dearly and she butted in before Grandfather Russell could respond to the offer.

"Thomas Russell,"

she said sharply,

"You shall never have that field."

And he never did.

32. MR. WILLIAM ASTON'S LARGESSE

When I was about 16 or 17 years of age and articled to a prominent firm of local surveyors and estate agents in Wolverhampton, Mr. William Aston, the Squire's brother, asked me to cash a cheque for him when I was in town.

This would save Mr. Aston a special trip to the bank and he would still be able to pay his men in cash at the end of the week as usual. I was young enough to be flattered to be asked by one of the village gentry to take on this responsibility and replied that I would be very pleased to do it.

I went to Mr. Aston's bank on the following day and drew out the money, which was a sizeable amount of cash for those days.

On returning home that evening, I went around to Mr. Aston's large house and handed him the stout paper bag containing the cash. He counted it carefully twice to make sure that the correct amount of money had been collected.

When Mr. Aston was satisfied, he turned to me and said,

"Russell, I would like to show my appreciation to you for fetching this money for me and for saving me all the trouble of going to the bank."

Mr. Aston reached into his pocket and drew out a coin.

"Russell" he said again,

"Would you know what to do with sixpence?"

At that point I was suddenly reminded for some reason of my distant cousin, 'Ready-Money Tom' and his son Jesse!

33. MR. ASTON'S FOREMAN – GREGORY'S BACON

Mr. William Aston employed a handyman-foreman called Dick Gregory, on whom he depended a lot for work around the house and farm buildings. One of Gregory's jobs was to keep an eye on the condition of the hams and sides of bacon, which were prepared for use in the following winter and spring.

These were hung from the ceiling in a cool pantry.

Now when Gregory felt like a bit of decent ham or bacon for his own family, he would say to his employer,

"I'm afraid, sir, that the ham in the far comer of the pantry is going a bit off."

In such cases, Mr. Aston would invariably reply,

"Oh, all right, Gregory, you had better take it home then."

Gregory never argued.

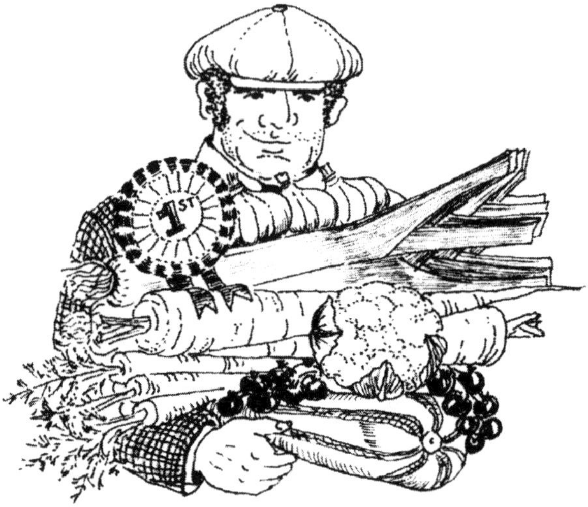
1ST

34. THE VILLAGE FLOWER AND VEGETABLE SHOW

Dick Gregory used to exhibit his flowers and vegetables at the village show each year. He nearly always won several of the major prizes.

However, Mr. William Aston, his employer, who entered the same competitions, rarely won any prize.

One day Mr. Aston said to Gregory,

''I don't know how it is, but each year we show our vegetables and flowers at the village show and you always beat me. How do you do it?"

Gregory did not answer, but smiled inwardly. As he told a friend afterwards, the answer to Mr. Aston's question was really quite simple.

You see he could always beat his employer because he had the choice of the best flowers and vegetables from both his own garden and his employer's.

35. CROSSING THE BRIDGE

Dick Gregory was quite a character. In addition to being the chief handyman to Mr. William Aston he was also Honorary Secretary to one of the local working men's clubs, which used to meet at the Seven Stars public house on the first Monday of each month. On occasions the club members had the odd drink during the meetings. Or so I am told.

One evening he left the meeting in a rather inebriated condition and started to walk through the village to his home.

He later told my father that, when he had to cross the tiny, hump-backed bridge over the little stream that divided the village, he was so unsteady on his feet that he had to get down on his hands and knees in order to negotiate the steep hill in the middle of the bridge.

He said he could never understand this, because he had never before been scared of heights.

36. GREGORY'S VISIT TO THE BALLET

Mr. William Aston really had quite a kindly heart and sometimes, as a special treat, took one or two of his employees to London on the train to see a cricket match and to see some of the sights.

On one occasion he invited Dick Gregory, his handyman-foreman, to go with him. Now Gregory had hardly crossed the parish boundary previously and the visit to London was indeed a day of wonderment for him.

After the cricket match at Lord's the pair went to the ballet, which was quite unlike anything that Gregory had seen before in his whole life.

A day or two later, when Gregory had taken up his usual position at the bar of the Seven Stars, the landlord said to him,

"Dick, I believe you went to the ballet when you were in London. How did you like it?"

Gregory replied,

"I didn't see any bally, but I saw lots of legs."

I should point out that, in our particular part of the world, the locals referred to a 'belly of pork' as a 'bally of pork.'

37. THE THATCHERS

Mr. William Aston used to employ the same two itinerant workers each summer to thatch his haystacks so that his valuable hay crop could be protected from the weather until it was needed for his animals.

It was his policy always to provide these workers with enough beer to help them carry out this hot and tiring task.

On one occasion, Mr. Aston's man, Gregory, was unable to find the wooden beer barrel which was normally kept charged with beer for the thatchers. The local brewery was asked to provide a replacement barrel filled with beer at very short notice.

Dick Gregory, who went to collect the new barrel from the brewery, reported to Mr. Aston that, because of the short notice, a barrel that had previously contained cherry brandy was the only one available. Mr. Aston could see no difficulty in this, provided that the brewery had filled it with their best beer.

As he usually did at thatching time, Gregory filled some bottles with beer from the new barrel for the thatchers to take with them into the fields.

Later that day, Mr. Aston thought that he should go to see how the thatchers were progressing with their work. When he got down to the field containing the haystack on which they were working Mr. Aston could not see any movement on or near the stack. He thought this strange, because the two men were steady workers who could be relied on to complete the work in hand as quickly and effectively as possible.

As he went round to the far side of the stack, he was surprised to find the two thatchers lying motionless beside their pitchforks, surrounded by a collection of empty bottles. It soon became obvious to Mr. Aston that the two men were dead drunk.

He lifted one of the bottles to his nose and sniffed. He suddenly realised what must have happened. He was as sure as could be that the new beer barrel had not been completely empty of cherry brandy when it was filled with beer at the brewery.

Gregory thought that he had better test his master's theory, so he took home with him that evening several bottles filled from the barrel, to see if the contents really were as strong as they appeared to be.

38. PUDGE

Several of the local farmers each winter employed a particular itinerant worker, named Pudge, to pick Brussels sprouts, when the snow and frost was about.

Nobody else wanted to do this job in the freezing cold, but Pudge was happy to earn a few shillings in this way, no matter how cold it was, or how much snow covered the ground. He worked hard and earned quite good money for those days.

After three or four days work, when he had some good wages to draw, he would stop work for a few days and would then spend his time propping up the bar at the Seven Stars until his money was gone.

When he was in his cups, he got very pugnacious and was always looking for a fight.

On one such occasion, after several hours solid drinking, Pudge got into an argument in the bar of the Seven Stars with another itinerant worker who was just passing through the village.

This inevitably resulted in the need for a scrap, so outside the pub they went for a fight.

When the fists had been flying for several minutes, it was obvious to the crowd of onlookers that Pudge, on this occasion, was on the receiving end.

In order to encourage their own local pugilist, Dick Gregory and the crowd cheered him on.

'Stop him, Pudge, Stop him," they shouted repeatedly.

To the uninitiated, I should explain that in boxing circles "Stop him" means "Knock him out."

However, Pudge was obviously mystified by this exhortation and he stopped fighting and glared at his pals.

"I can't stop him, because I ain't seen him go by yet," he growled through bruised lips.

Neither did he see the knockout punch coming!

39. THE RIGHT TURN OF PHRASE

One fine October day, Mr. William Aston was going round one of his farms to see how work on the autumn cultivation was progressing. He came to a field in which one of his men, Jack (a distant cousin of Dick Gregory), was ploughing using a team of three horses.

Mr. Aston waited at the top end of the field until Jack and his horses came up and made ready to turn the plough round to go down again. The Squire's brother beckoned his man across to ask him how the ploughing was going.

After discussing the state of the land and what the weather was going to do during the next few days, Mr. Aston told Jack to carry on with the good work.

Jack returned to his team of horses and flicked the reins.

"Get on! Get on!" he shouted to the horses. Nothing happened. The horses did not move.

"Get on! Move!" he shouted even more loudly, his weather-beaten face going an even darker colour. Still the horses did not move; not even a muscle twitched.

Mr. Aston realised that he would have to do something to help.

"Jack," he said, "Speak to them as if I wasn't here."

Jack nodded and said to the horses in a much quieter tone,

"Come on, you buggers,"

.... and off the horses went down the field, contentedly pulling the plough.

40. A SITTING OF EGGS

This final story illustrates my father's strong, disciplinary nature.

When I was about ten years old, I remember that a distant relative used to come over to Home Farm from Wolverhampton each week in his pony and trap to collect eggs for his family.

On one of these occasions, I was sent to another part of the farm to fetch a 'sitting' (about a dozen) of eggs from Fred Gittins, who looked after the chickens. When I got there, after a hot walk in the afternoon sun, Gittins placed the eggs carefully on a soft, white cloth in a basket, so that they could be carried easily and safely back to the farmhouse.

I set off homewards in high spirits, because the relative usually gave me a silver sixpence for fetching his eggs, so I was in a hurry to get home and collect my reward.

So I started to run, watching the eggs in the basket carefully to make sure that they would come to no harm. To save even more time, I went through a hole in the hedge at the side of the track to take a short cut across the fields. Almost immediately, my foot caught in a rabbit hole and I fell headlong onto the hard, sun-baked ground.

The eggs were all thrown out of the basket and every one was smashed. I was frightened, because I knew that there would be terrible trouble for being so clumsy.

I, therefore, decided to hide all the evidence of this terrible accident and stuffed the broken eggs down the rabbit hole and hid the basket with its cloth in the hedge bottom. I then walked slowly and dejectedly towards the farmhouse on the far horizon.

When I finally got home, father said,

"Ernie, where are the eggs?"

I replied,

"I'm sorry, father. They didn't have any today."

"Oh," said my father,

"That's strange."

and he apologised to his visitor for his wasted journey.

I heard nothing further about this unhappy episode for two days and was beginning to think that I would avoid retribution after all.

My father called out for me just before dinnertime on the second day. He had evidently just asked Fred Gittins why on the day before yesterday there had been no eggs. Gittins had replied, of course, that there had indeed been some eggs and that the boy had come to collect a sitting.

Without waiting for an explanation, my father took hold of me by the scruff of the neck, and proceeded to kick my bottom all the way up the stairs to his bedroom.

I remember being left without my dinner, with time to reflect on my wrongdoing until the next morning.

No explanation was ever given for this severe punishment, but I knew exactly why I had received it.

It was a long time before I told another lie to anyone.

APPENDIX

The story of the stories

During his later years 'Ernie' Russell wrote extensively about his life. However in the tradition of oral storytelling the stories in this book were recorded on to cassette tape and have since been transcribed. This is the first time his 'tales' have been written down, but we know from history that the best storytellers tended to 'borrow' good stories from others.

An engaging story often has the listener pondering the question: 'truth' or 'tale'? Some of them are rather difficult to believe. In preparing this book for publication I was very surprised to find a photo of a plaque regarding the Mr George Pudsey Aston-Pudsey mentioned in one of the stories. It seemed that some of the most unlikely stories I was told as a child were most likely true!

Evidence of the person George Pudsey Aston-Pudsey in Tale No. 6 'The Aston Family'

'Ernie' had clearly told these stories to others, including my father, as he thought they should be preserved in some way. In the 1970s, whilst his father was living in a residential care home, my father recorded 'Ernie' on a cassette tape. I am fortunate to have the unedited, original recordings and also having my father's 'prompt' cards in preparation for that conversation which show that he, too, was very well acquainted with the stories.

The scan of one prompt card is for 'The Thatchers', Tale No. 37 and 'The Colonel', Tale No. 15, which indicate that father and son both knew the task ahead of them. The tapes were not edited at the time and when I reviewed them it was clear that my grandfather required few prompts at any stage.

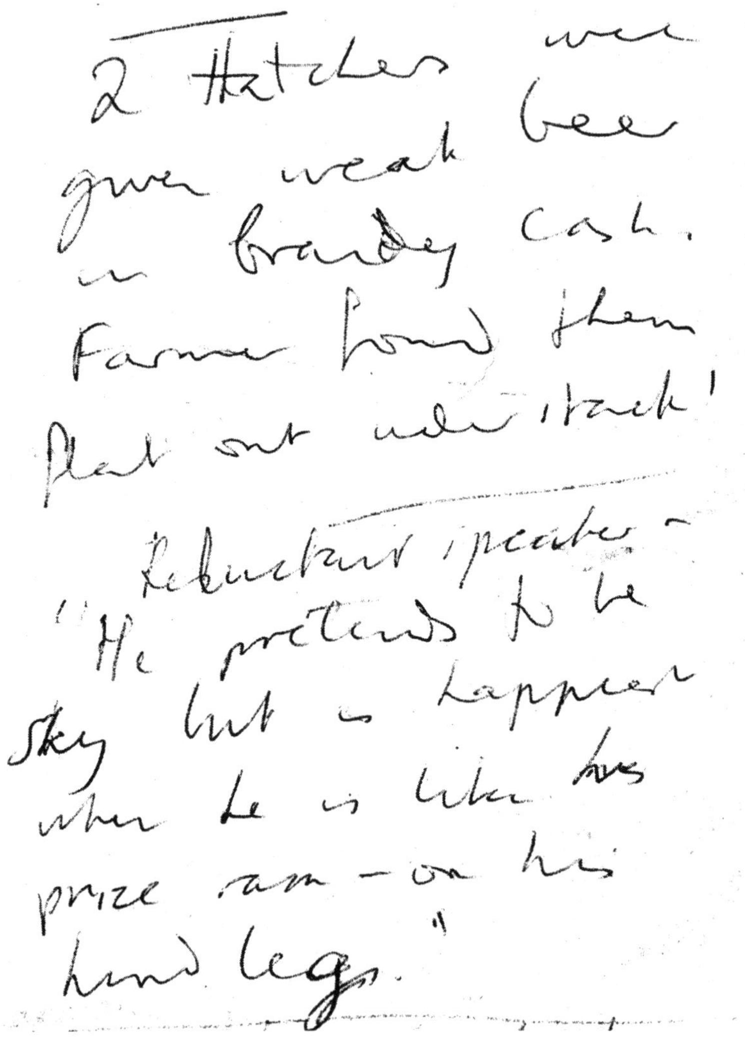
2 Thatchers were given weak beer in brandy cask. Farmer found them flat out under stack!

Reluctant speaker – "He pretends to be shy but is happier when he is like his prize ram – on his hind legs."

Prompt card for Tale No. 37 'The Thatchers' and Tale No. 15 'The Colonel'

From the recordings, my father made handwritten transcriptions:

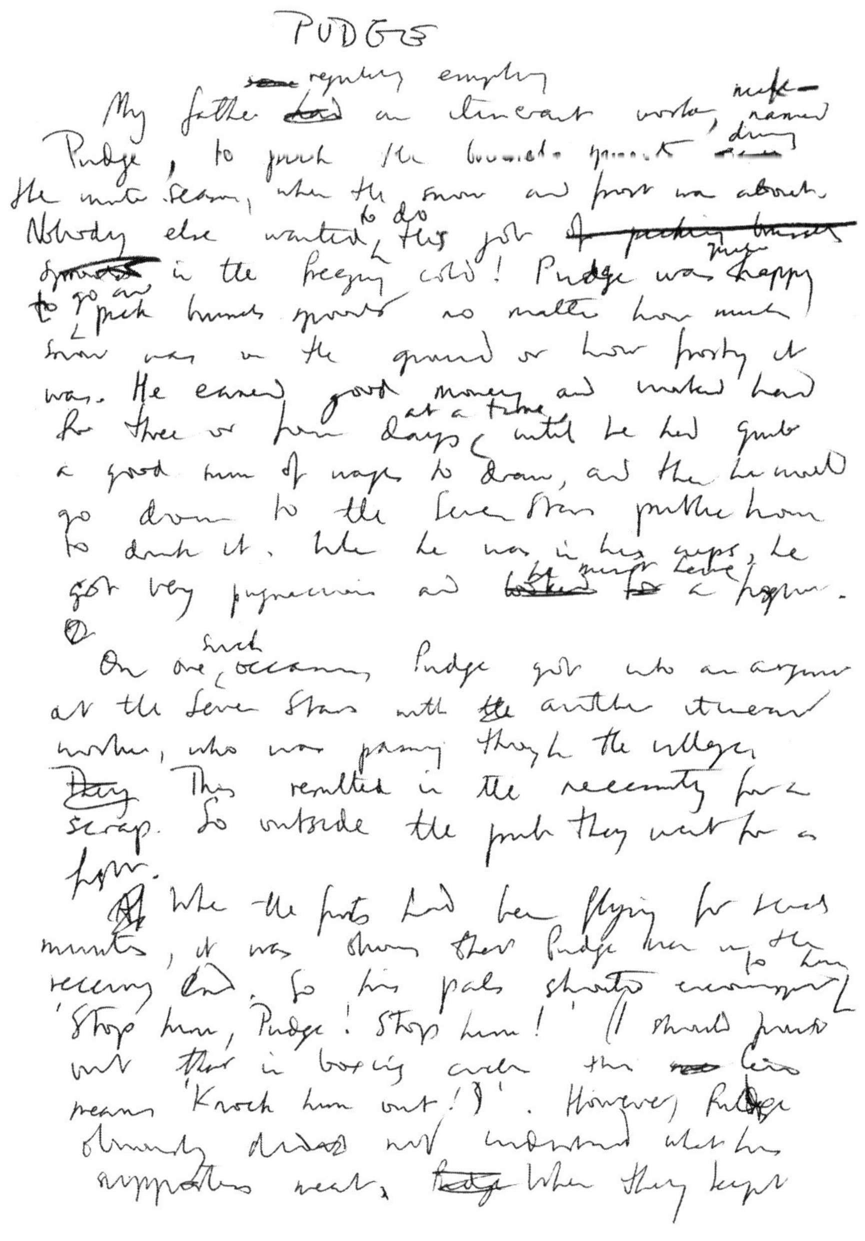
PUDGE

My father regularly employed an itinerant worker, nicknamed Pudge, to pick the brussels sprouts during the winter season, when the snow and frost was about. Nobody else wanted to do this job in the freezing cold! Pudge was happy to go and pick brussels sprouts no matter how much snow was on the ground or how frosty it was. He earned good money and worked hard for three or four days at a time, until he had quite a good sum of wages to draw, and then he would go down to the Seven Stars public house to drink it. When he was in his cups, he got very pugnacious and he might seek a fight.

On one such occasion Pudge got into an argument at the Seven Stars with another itinerant worker, who was passing through the village. This resulted in the necessity for a scrap. So outside the pub they went for a fight.

When the fists had been flying for several minutes, it was obvious that Pudge was on the receiving end. So his pals shouted to him encouragingly 'Stop him, Pudge! Stop him!' (I should point out that in boxing circles this term means 'Knock him out!'). However, Pudge obviously did not understand what his supporters meant, when they kept

Transcription of Tale No. 38 'Pudge!'

before keying them to a data file on what is now a very primitive computer, with a continuous paper dot matrix printer. This photo shows that this part was closely supervised by his cat, 'Tigger'.

Tigger!

There are some discrepancies between some character names in the transcribed tales to those I remember hearing as a child. When compiling the book of tales, I was able to listen to the audio files to confirm this. For example, the following sample transcriptions refer to 'George Ashorth Pudsey'.

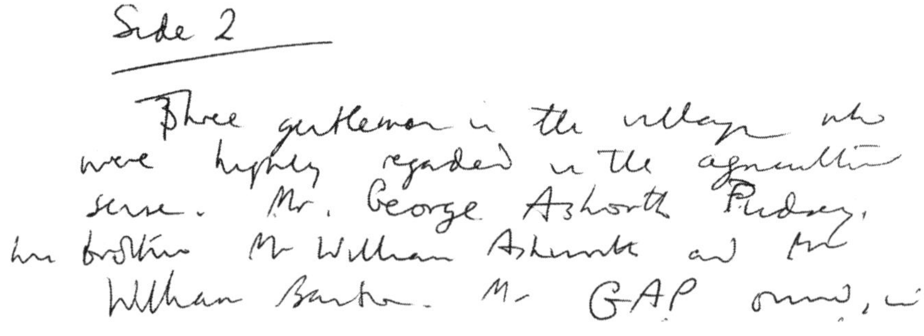

Side 2

Three gentlemen in the village who were highly regarded in the agricultural sense. Mr. George Ashorth Pudsey, his brother Mr William Ashworth and Mr William Barton. Mr GAP owned, in

Transcription of Tale No. 5 'Some Village People'

Another example from the transcription is Ernie's schoolmaster being called 'John Troutbeck' and in the audio files he was clearly 'John Salmon'. The name differences seem deliberate and I have attributed the differences to my father's sensitivity to anyone who might have been alive at the time and also to the laws on slander/libel. On the basis that none of the tales were intended to be a factual description of village life and in no way to offend, I have listened to the tapes and returned to the original names 'Ernie' used.

Following his retirement from his role as Professor of Agricultural Biology at The University of Newcastle Upon Tyne, UK, my father took up publishing in the STM (Scientific Technical & Medical) sector, but he clearly intended for his father's oral storytelling to be published, as he sketched out what the front cover would look like.

Cover design based on Tale No. 9 'Trapped!'

He also commissioned three pen and ink drawings to illustrate the tales (the artist is unknown and this is the only image that has survived).

Tale No. 7 Mr William Barton ('Parrot and Cage')

Gordon Russell's sudden, premature death meant he was unable to complete the book, so in the best traditions of storytelling and as one of the last generations to have heard these tales first hand, this is their work completed.

I hope readers will agree that the illustrations in this book are far superior to the above. The illustrations in Edwardian Village Tales began as an inspired Christmas present commissioned by my wife Izzy, who had a University friend who is a most talented artist. Later she agreed to illustrate them all.

Janet Watson, our illustrator, has already introduced herself, but seeing the illustrations as they arrived over a few months took me back on an emotional yet healing journey – back to childhood, sitting on my grandfather's knee, waiting, anticipating, which of these 40 plus stories he would tell that day.

I hope you enjoyed reading these stories.

Andrew Russell

ACKNOWLEDGMENTS

To the late Professor (Emeritus) Gordon Russell for his foresight and hard work to capture his father's tales on cassette tape for posterity.

To Janet Watson, who worked so professionally to illustrate the stories with so much skill and imagination.

To Jeremy Lodge, my friend of over 44 years for his important advice on printing and publishing.

To my wife Izzy for her patience in checking the book for errors and omissions.

To the friends and relatives in Canada, many of whom are descendants of family from the UK villages whence the tales originate, who gave me encouragement and energy to preserve them for current and future generations.

"It's not magic that takes us to another world. It's storytelling."

Val McDermid (Scottish crime writer)

There are 5 publications in this series, but they are also stand-alone paperback titles.

This book is:

Edwardian Village Tales: told by "Ernie" Russell, illustrated by Janet Watson, edited by Andrew Russell
ISBN 978-1-9160441-2-8 234 x 156mm (UK Royal), 102 printed pages, over 40 commissioned pen and ink illustrations by Janet Watson, November 2019.

Other titles:

My early life in Pattingham, Trysull and Seisdon (Staffordshire). 1893–1913: "Ernie" Russell
ISBN 978-1-9160441-1-1 c. 60 printed pages, A5 Paperback, publication mid-2020.

A Private Soldier's views on the Great War 1914–1918. "Ernie" Russell, compiled by Andrew Russell, with illustrations by Janet Watson
ISBN 978-1-9160441-0-4 A5 paperback, c. 148 printed pages, publication late January 2020.

Becoming an early 20th Century pioneer. Family emigration to Canada and homesteading in Saskatchewan: "Ernie" Russell
ISBN 978-1-9160441-3-5 A5 paperback, c. 64 printed pages with illustrations by Janet Watson, publication November 2020. This title will be launched in Saskatchewan, Canada, but available worldwide.

Reflections on 40 years as a land agent in Bedfordshire 1921–1958: "Ernie" Russell
ISBN 978-1-9160441-4-2 A5 paperback, c. 106 printed pages, publication late June 2020.

All titles available from Andrew Russell, Intercept Publishers, 5 Upsall Cottages, Guisborough, TS14 6RP. Tel. (44) 07888739054
(email: interceptpublishers@gmail.com for price details or to be sent a PayPal payment link), or available from good bookshops who can take alternative methods of payment.